DICK KING-SMITH
All Because of Jackson

Also available by Dick King-Smith,
and published by Doubleday:

THE GUARD DOG
HORSE PIE
CONNIE AND ROLLO
HARRIET'S HARE
OMNIBOMBULATOR
HAPPY MOUSEDAY

Picture books:

JUNGLE JINGLES AND OTHER
ANIMAL POEMS
illustrated by Jonathan Allen

HORACE AND MAURICE
illustrated by Sami Sweeten

DICK KING-SMITH

All Because of
Jackson

Illlustrated by

John Eastwood

DOUBLEDAY

LONDON . NEW YORK . TORONTO . SYDNEY . AUCKLAND

TRANSWORLD PUBLISHERS LTD
61–63 Uxbridge Road, London W5 5SA

TRANSWORLD PUBLISHERS (AUSTRALIA) PTY LTD
15–25 Helles Avenue, Moorebank, NSW 2170

TRANSWORLD PUBLISHERS (NZ) LTD
3 William Pickering Drive, Albany, Auckland

DOUBLEDAY CANADA LTD
105 Bond Street, Toronto, Ontario M5B 1Y3

Published 1995 by Doubleday
a division of Transworld Publishers Ltd

A catalogue record for this book is available
from the British Library

ISBN 0 385 40598 7

Typeset in 20/26pt Bembo Schoolbook
by Phoenix Typesetting, Ilkley, West Yorkshire

Printed and bound in Great Britain by
Mackays of Chatham PLC, Chatham, Kent

CONTENTS

CHAPTER ONE

Jackson was a seaside rabbit.

He was born in a sandy burrow on top of a cliff, and as soon as he was old enough to come out and sit on the grass and look down at the sea, he was fascinated by it.

While his brothers and sisters played about in the clifftop field, Jackson would sit by himself and watch the waves rolling in to break upon the sandy shore.

He watched the tides go in and out, he watched the seabirds wheeling and diving, and especially he watched the tall sailing-ships gliding past in the distance. How beautiful they are, thought Jackson. How I should love to run away to sea and be a sailor.

He consulted his mother.

'Mama,' he said.

'Yes, Jackson?'

'There are men on those ships, aren't there?'

'Yes, Jackson. Sailors.'

'I should like to be a sailor, Mama.'

'Silly boy,' said Jackson's mother. 'Rabbits don't go on ships.'

'But Mama, the sea is in my blood.'

'You go on a ship,' said his mother, 'and your blood will be in the sea. Men eat rabbits.'

Jackson went away to think about this. I could hide, he thought. There must be lots of places to hide in a big sailing-ship. I could be a stowaway. I won't tell Mama or Papa. I'll just go.

So he did.

He set off across the clifftop field very early one morning, determined to find where the sailing-ships came in. That evening, climbing wearily to the top of a far headland, he looked down and saw before him just what he wanted.

There below was a wide bay,

and on its shores a large seaside
town with a great harbour, in
which lay a number of tall ships.

Tired out, Jackson found an
empty rabbit burrow and
crawled into it.

'Tomorrow,' he murmured as
he drifted into sleep, 'tomorrow I
shall go aboard my ship.'

CHAPTER TWO

That night Jackson had the
weirdest dream.

He was, it seemed, in a
strange country, not cool and
rainy like his homeland, but dry
and very hot. Suddenly he saw
the most extraordinary animal.

It was as tall as a man, with
reddish fur, ears like a donkey,
and a face like a sheep. Its arms
were short, and it stood upright,
balanced upon two enormously
strong legs and a long, thick tail.
Then the dream turned into a
nightmare, for the monstrous

creature began to come towards him, not walking, not running, but hopping in huge bounds on those great hind legs. And as it drew near, Jackson could see something even more frightening. On the animal's stomach was a sort of pocket, and out of this pocket poked another head, with ears like a baby donkey and a face like a lamb!

Jackson woke with a squeal of terror.

'What's eating you?' said a
voice, and there beside him in
the burrow was another rabbit, a
young doe of about his own
age.

'I was having a bad dream,'
he said.

'In my burrow,' said the other.

'Oh, sorry!' said Jackson. 'I
didn't know. By the way, my
name's Jackson.'

'Funny sort of name.'

'Not really. My father's called Jack. Anyway, who are you?'

'My mother doesn't believe in naming children,' said the young doe. 'She's had so many, she can't be bothered. She just calls us all "Bunny".'

'Bunny?' said Jackson. 'That's nice. I like it.' And I like you, he thought. I wonder if . . .

'You don't fancy going to sea, do you, Bunny?' he said.

'To sea?'

'In a ship. To sail away over the ocean.'

'Where to?' said Bunny.

'I don't know,' replied
Jackson. 'That'll be half the fun
of it, not knowing.'

'But rabbits don't go on ships,'
said Bunny.

'This one's going to,' said
Jackson. 'I want to sail the seas.
I want to see the world.'

'You're crazy,' Bunny said.
But nice, she thought.

'Well,' she said, 'it'll be
daylight before very long. We'd
better get started.'

When they reached the town,
Jackson and Bunny hopped
through the empty silent streets
until, as dawn was breaking,
they reached the docks.

'Look!' cried Jackson as they
made their way along the
cobbled quay. 'There's a ship!'

Tied up alongside was a great
three-masted sailing-ship, whose
sides towered above the two little
rabbits.

'How ever shall we get aboard?' said Bunny.

'The same way that the sailors do,' said Jackson. 'Follow me!' And he ran along the quay until he reached the foot of a long, narrow, wooden gangplank. It was nearly broad daylight by now and there were noises on board, bangings and knockings and men's voices and footsteps.

'Quick!' said Jackson. 'Up we go!' And up they went, scampering up the gangplank on whose side was fixed a large printed notice.

Brave British Hearts!
To all those of an
Adventurous Spirit
wishing to seek their fortunes and start a new life in a far country, take note that the Peninsular & Oriental Navigation Company's Clipper
Atalanta
will set sail for
AUSTRALIA
on the
Third day of April 1842

CHAPTER THREE

The moment that Jackson and
Bunny reached the top of the
gangplank, they saw to their
horror a number of sailors busy
swabbing down the decks.
Luckily the men's backs were
towards the two rabbits, who
instantly dashed for cover.

A frightened rabbit goes
straight underground, and
though here there was no
ground to go under, Jackson
saw nearby a large,
square, black
hole,

and into it he dived head first,
Bunny following. Down the
hatch they fell.

As well as passengers, the
Atalanta was carrying in her hold
goods for the settlers in Australia,
and, luckily for the rabbits (for
they fell a long way), it was a
cargo of bales of cloth. On these
Jackson and Bunny landed and
bounced.

'Are you all right, Bunny?'
gasped Jackson.

'Yes, I think so. Where are
we?'

'In a very big burrow by the
look of things,' said Jackson. 'A
good place for us to stow away,
I should think.'

'Would you?' said Bunny.

'Well, yes. We can hide
amongst all this stuff. No-one
will ever find us. We can spend
the whole voyage down here.'

'And at the end of the voyage,'
said Bunny, 'how exactly do we
get out again?'   Jackson looked
up at the open hatch, high
above. He scratched one ear
thoughtfully with a hind foot.

'Ah,' he said.

'And while we're down here,'
went on Bunny, 'what exactly
do we eat?'

'Ah,' said Jackson again.

'Or drink?'

'Ah,' said Jackson. 'Yes. Hm.'
But before he could add to this,
they heard the sound of footsteps
on the deck above, and voices,
and then suddenly the square of

daylight vanished as the hatch cover was put back, leaving the hold of the ship in darkness.

'It had better be a very short voyage,' said Bunny. 'Otherwise it would seem to me that, without food or water, we shall not see much of the world after all. We shall simply die down here. And all because of you, Jackson.'

All that morning the two rabbits hopped about in the gloom, exploring the great stack of bales of cloth that covered the floor of the hold, and finding nothing else.

Above them, there was much hustle and bustle on deck as the passengers came aboard, and then, around midday, a sudden great crash of sound as a brass band struck up on the quayside.

In amongst its noise the
rabbits could hear voices
bellowing orders, and the cries of
farewell of those who were
leaving and of those who had
come to wave them goodbye.

Then, when the music had
stopped and the shouts and calls
had died away, peace and quiet
returned as the *Atalanta* nosed
her way out of harbour, and set
sail for her journey to the
opposite side of the world.

Down in the hold, Jackson
and Bunny felt the motion as the
clipper met the open sea, and
heard the creaking of her
timbers. Squatting side by side
on a bale of cloth, the rabbits
rose and fell as the ship swooped
and dipped over the waves.

'Jackson,' said Bunny.

'Yes?'

'I don't feel very well.'

'Me neither.'

'I don't think I'm a very good sailor.'

'Nor me.'

'I wish I hadn't come.'

'Me too,' said Jackson. 'I'm sorry I got you into all this, Bunny. It's all my fault. I shall regret it for the rest of my life.'

Bunny snuggled up to him. 'Don't worry,' she said. 'That won't be long.'

By the following day the rabbits had grown used to the motion of the ship. They had also grown extremely hungry and thirsty.

When the ship had been some days at sea, the captain ordered an inspection of the various holds, to see that each was watertight and that their cargo had not shifted.

By now too weak and miserable to care, the rabbits watched helplessly as the hatch cover was removed, and a seaman climbed down a ladder, carrying a lantern.

A big, bearded man, he shone
the light about as he examined
the bales of cloth, and then its
beam fell full upon the wretched
stowaways.

'Well, I never!' said the
seaman softly. 'You'll make a
nice meal, my hearties, you will!'

Afterwards, Jackson and Bunny couldn't really remember what happened, so weak and helpless were they.

In fact, the bearded seaman found a sack and popped them in it, and climbed the ladder out of the hold, only to meet the first mate at the hatchway.

'All shipshape down below, Jenkins?' said the mate.

'Aye, aye, sir,' replied Jenkins.

'What have you got in that sack?'

The seaman heaved a sigh.

He'll have 'em off me, he
thought, that's for sure.

'Rabbits, sir,' he said.

'Rabbits?' said the mate.

'Yes, sir,' said Jenkins. 'Found
'em in among the bales. Don't
know how they come to be there.'

The mate opened the mouth
of the sack and peered in.

'Well, well!' he said. 'They'll
make a nice meal. Take them
down to the galley and tell the
cook I'll have them for my supper.'

'Aye, aye, sir,' said Jenkins dolefully, but before he could move, the captain of the *Atalanta* appeared, an imposing figure with mutton-chop whiskers, a gold-peaked cap upon his head, and a brass telescope under his arm.

'What's all this, Mister Mate?' he said. 'What has that man got in that sack?'

The first mate heaved a sigh. He'll have 'em off me, he thought, that's certain.

'Rabbits, sir,' he said.

'Rabbits?' said the captain.

'Yes, sir,' said the mate. 'Open the sack, Jenkins.'

'Well, well,' said the captain. 'I'm very partial to a nice young rabbit, or better still, two nice young rabbits, under a good, light, pastry crust, with some strips of fat bacon.'

He put a hand into the sack and felt the limp forms within.

'Found 'em down below, did you, Jenkins?' he said.

'Yes, sir.'

'Heaven only knows how they got there,' said the captain, 'but one thing's sure. They'll have had no food or water since we sailed. They're as weak as kittens. We must put some flesh on them first. Jenkins, take them to my cabin steward and tell him to see to their needs.'

'Aye, aye, sir,' said the seaman.

'And Mister Mate,' said the captain, 'I'd be obliged if you'd have a word with the ship's carpenter. Tell him to knock me up a cage for my rabbits, and to bring it up to my cabin when it's done.'

'Aye, aye, sir,' said the mate.

'One thing's sure,' said the captain. 'Once my rabbits have grown a bit and fattened up, they'll be well worth waiting for. I shall enjoy them, Mister Mate. They'll make a nice meal.'

By great good fortune, the captain's cabin steward was a rabbit fancier. Ashore, he kept a shed full of tame ones, and under his expert care Jackson and Bunny soon recovered their health and strength.

Amongst the stores of food that the *Atalanta* had loaded for her voyage was a plentiful supply of vegetables, still fresh, and the two young rabbits gorged happily on cabbage-leaves and carrot-tops and turnip-greens.

In addition, the steward fed
them broken bits of ship's biscuit,
and generally looked after them
very well. In due course, he
knew, the captain would eat
them, but that was what rabbits
were for.

'Tuck in, my dears,' he said,
stroking their brown backs.
'Enjoy life while you can.'

And indeed they did.

'It's funny, you know,' said
Jackson to Bunny. 'Mama told
me that men eat rabbits, but that

doesn't seem to be true.'

'They're certainly treating us well,' said Bunny with her mouth full. 'Both the little one who feeds us and the big one with the whiskers who stands and stares at us. I'm really quite enjoying this voyage now.'

'Me too,' said Jackson. 'I wonder where we shall end up?'

In the captain's pie-dish was of course the answer to this question, and some weeks later the cabin steward's expert advice was sought.

'You keep rabbits at home,
     Tompkins, don't ye?'
     said the captain.
     'Yes, sir.'
'What d'ye think of these two
now? Fit to eat, would you say?'
'Well, sir,' said the steward,
'they're not yet fully grown. I
don't reckon they were more
than two month old when they
come aboard. And we've been at
sea eight weeks – that makes
'em four month old now.'
'Another four weeks' sailing,'
said the captain, 'and we'll reach
Australia. I want to make a
meal of them before then.'

'Was you going to eat the both of them yourself, sir?' asked the steward.

I was, thought the captain, when they were littler, but now . . . maybe I should give a little dinner, for Sir Hereward and his lady, with rabbit-pie as the main course.

Sir Hereward Potts was a rich and important merchant in the city of London, sailing to Australia with the intention of becoming the richest and most important merchant in the city of Sydney. He was much the most notable of the *Atalanta's* passengers. A favourable report to the Peninsular and Oriental Navigation Company from Sir Hereward Potts would do the captain no harm at all, and the rabbit-pie would do Sir Hereward a power of good.

'Eat both of them myself, Tompkins?' said the captain in reply to the steward's question. 'Of course not. I shall invite Sir Hereward and Lady Potts to share such a treat.'

That evening the captain of the *Atalanta* asked the merchant and his wife to his cabin for a glass of wine, and proposed the little dinner party.

'Tomorrow, at about this hour?' he said. That should give Tompkins ample time to see to the preparation of the pie, he thought.

'Delighted, Captain,' said Sir Hereward.

'Too kind,' said Lady Potts.

Then she caught sight of
Jackson and Bunny, lolloping
happily about in their cage.

'Oh!' she cried. 'How I do
love rabbits!'

'So do I,' said the captain.
'They are to be the main
attraction of our little dinner
tomorrow. They are still young
and should be very tender, I
have no doubt.'

Much to the captain's surprise,
Lady Potts gave a little scream
of horror.

'Oh, Captain!' she cried. 'Oh,
you could not! Surely you do
not mean to kill those charming

little creatures? Oh, I could not
bear to think of such a thing,
much less eat them. Oh,
Hereward, must they be slain?'

'My wife is tender-hearted,
Captain,' said Sir Hereward, and
he did not look best pleased.

The captain thought fast.
'I do apologize for suggesting
such a thing, your Ladyship,' he
said. 'I had not realized . . . so
thoughtless of me.'

Stupid woman, he thought,
now I shan't be able to eat
them, she'll be for ever asking
me how they are. There's only
one thing to do.

'Sir Hereward,' he said with a
little bow, 'I wonder – would
you permit me to present these
animals to Lady Potts as a gift,
in token of my esteem?'

Sir Hereward looked doubtful.

'The rabbit is unknown in Australia,' went on the captain, 'and the possession of these two specimens would be in keeping with your wife's position as a leader in colonial society.'

Lady Potts gave another little scream, this time of delight, and cried, 'Yes! Oh, Captain, yes, how kind of you. Pray have them removed to our quarters for the remainder of the voyage. We shall be delighted to have them, shall we not, Hereward?'

And though Sir Hereward Potts' word was law to thousands in the world of business, he knew better than to cross swords with his wife.

'Yes, my dear,' he said. 'Delighted.'

Thus it was that for the remaining four weeks of the voyage of the *Atalanta* to the Antipodes, the stowaways found themselves in the lap of luxury. Jackson and Bunny were petted and fondled and fed upon the choicest of titbits, and allowed the freedom of the Potts' stateroom for much of the day,

while, with dustpan and brush, a
steward cleaned up behind them.

When at last, at the end of
her three-month voyage, the
clipper *Atalanta* entered Sydney
Harbour, the rabbits were in
beautiful condition: fat, sleek and
strong.

Sir Hereward had taken a house in the country, some way outside Sydney, and to this he travelled by coach with his wife and all their many pieces of baggage. Among these was the rabbit cage, covered with a sheet to conceal the inmates from prying eyes, for Lady Potts intended to surprise the colonials with her unusual pets.

When they arrived she insisted that the rabbit cage be unloaded first and placed upon the lawn.

'I must let my little friends stretch their legs,' she said to her husband, and she removed the sheet and opened the door of the cage.

Jackson and Bunny hopped out and looked about them.

'We seem to have arrived,' said Jackson.

'But where?' said Bunny.

'I have no idea.'

'Will they not run away, my dear?' said Sir Hereward.

'Run away?' said Lady Potts. 'What an idea! They are much too tame and much too fond of me, are you not, my dears?' And she bent to stroke them.

'Bunny,' said Jackson. 'Are you thinking what I'm thinking?'

'Yes,' said Bunny. 'Let's go!' And side by side they raced away, the first rabbits ever to set foot upon Australian soil.

CHAPTER EIGHT

After all those months cooped up in the *Atalanta* it was sheer bliss to be out in the fresh air again, out in the sunshine (and very hot sunshine it was), and to be free once more.

Jackson and Bunny ran and ran, just for the joy of running, and leaped and twirled and buckjumped (or in Bunny's case doejumped) in the highest spirits, delighted with one another.

When at last they stopped and
looked about them, it was to see
a countryside very different from
their cool damp homeland. The
grass was more brown than
green, and the blue-gums looked

nothing like English trees. The
birds that they saw were strange
too – screeching cockatoos and
laughing kookaburras and flocks
of parrakeets and budgerigars.

Then suddenly Jackson saw a large shape in the distance.

'Quick! Hide!' he said to Bunny, and they scurried for the shelter of some tussocky grass.

'What's the matter?' said Bunny. 'You're trembling.'

'My dream!' said Jackson. 'Do you remember, when we first met in your burrow, I'd been having a bad dream?'

'Yes, I remember.'

'Well,' said Jackson, 'here it comes!' And peering through the grass stems, Bunny saw the most extraordinary animal.

It was as tall as a man, with reddish fur, ears like a donkey, and a face like a sheep. Its arms were short, and it stood upright, balanced upon two enormously strong legs and a long thick tail. Then this monstrous creature began to come towards them, not walking, not running, but hopping in huge bounds on those great hind legs. And as it drew near, Bunny could see something

even more frightening. On the
animal's stomach was a sort of
pocket, and out of this pocket
poked another head, with ears
like a baby donkey
and a face like
a lamb!

'Don't move,' whispered Jackson. 'It may not see us.' And the two rabbits froze, crouching low with ears laid flat back and eyes bulging with terror.

With one last hop the great red kangaroo landed right beside their hiding-place and looked down at them out of her mild sheep's eyes. From her pouch her joey looked down too.

'Ma,' he said. 'What kind of animals are those?'

'No idea, son,' said the mother kangaroo. 'Never seen such strange-looking creatures in my whole life. Hold tight now.'

And away she bounded.

'Fancy calling *us* strange!' said
Bunny. 'I never set eyes on such
weird things as those before.'

As time passed, Jackson and Bunny were to see a great many other odd-looking beasts. As well as kangaroos, they met wallabies and bandicoots and opossums and koalas and numbats and wombats and many more.

There were familiar creatures as well, like cattle and a great many sheep, but one sort of animal they never met.

'It's funny, isn't it?' said Jackson one day. 'In this place where we've landed up, wherever it is, there are no other rabbits.'

'No,' said Bunny, 'but there soon will be.'

'I don't understand,' said Jackson.

But a little later he did, for Bunny scratched herself a nest-burrow and there gave birth to five babies.

'Aren't they lovely!' said Jackson, and indeed, he must have liked babies, because by the end of the rabbits' first year in their new country, Bunny had produced four more litters, totalling twenty-two young in all, and by then she and Jackson were already great-grandparents!

After another year there were
hundreds of rabbits in Australia,
and then thousands, and then
tens of thousands.

Jackson and Bunny lived
happily (though not 'ever after',
because a rabbit's lifespan is not
a long one), and by the time
they died, peacefully, of old age,
there were hundreds of thousands
of rabbits. And before long there
were millions, and then countless

millions, that colonized large stretches of the best land in Australia; a great multitude of rabbits that dug holes everywhere and damaged trees and crops, and ate all the grass meant for the sheep, and drove the Australian settlers to distraction. One of the great plagues in the history of the world it was. And all because of Jackson.